Picture Perfect?

Written and illustrated by second grade students of Westwood Elementary Westwood, Calif.

Copyright © 2003 by Scholastic Inc
Scholastic and associated logos are trademarks and/or registered trademarks of Scholastic Inc
ISBN 0-439-61172-5

12 11 10 9 8 7 6 5 4 3 2 1   00 01 02 03 04

Book Design by Bill Henderson
Printed and bound in the U.S.A.

First Printing, July 2003

It's picture day at our school.

Everyone wants to look their best, but ...

My tooth came out.

I was angry.

I forgot to smile.

I got sick.

Mom picked my clothes.

I didn't comb my hair.

I got a perm.

My brother gave me a black eye.

I spilled spaghetti on my shirt.

Mom fixed my hair.

I lost a button.

My ears stuck out.

The cat scratched my face.

I had a milk mustache.

I cut my own hair.

The picture lady combed my hair.

I blinked.

I got braces yesterday.

I got into Mom's makeup.

I got a bloody nose.

I got a fat lip.

I got a cold sore.

But Dad will like it anyway!

Draw your own "Perfect Picture"!

Meet the Authors

Mrs. Costa

Alex Berry

Bodie Farris

Manaé Hackett

Josephine (JoJo) Keller

Danielle Kellum

Jeffery Lebert

Kimberley Marley

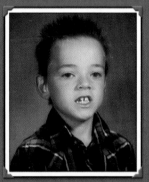

Clarence (Bubba) McArthur

Denis Obregon

Kellund Oldham

Brianna Ray

Destiny Richardson

Rayanne Rouse-Smith

Destiny Singleton

Tabatha Sterling

Asa Valentine

Ciera Valerga

Dustin Van Meter

Patrick West

Jimmy Worthington (not pictured)

Kids Are Authors ®
Books written by children for children

The Kids Are Authors ® Competition was established in 1986 to encourage children to read and to become involved in the creative process of writing. Since then, thousands of children have written and illustrated books as participants in the Kids Are Authors ® Competition. The winning books in the annual competition are published by Scholastic Inc. and are distributed by Scholastic Book Fairs throughout the United States.

For more information:
Kids Are Authors®
1080 Greenwood Blvd.
Lake Mary, FL 32746

Or visit our web site at:
www.scholastic.com/kidsareauthors